# AMAZING

# DRAGONS

# FIENDISH TALES OF DASTARDLY DEEDS

WRITTEN BY NICOLA BAXTER · ILLUSTRATED BY COLIN KING

ARMADILLO

This edition is published by Armadillo, an imprint of Anness Publishing Ltd,
Blaby Road, Wigston, Leicestershire LE18 4SE; info@anness.com

www.annesspublishing.com

If you like the images in this book and would like to investigate using them for publishing, promotions
or advertising, please visit our website www.practicalpictures.com for more information.

Publisher: Joanna Lorenz
Editors: Sally Delaney and Elizabeth Young
Designer: Amanda Hawkes
Production designer: Amy Barton
Production Controller: Don Campaniello

A CIP catalogue record for this book is available from the British Library.

PUBLISHER'S NOTE
Although the advice and information in this book are believed to be accurate and true at the time
of going to press, neither the authors nor the publisher can accept any legal responsibility or liability
for any errors or omissions that may have been made.

Manufacturer: Anness Publishing Ltd,
Blaby Road, Wigston, Leicestershire LE18 4SE, England
For Product Tracking go to: www.annesspublishing.com/tracking
Batch: 6062-20943-1127

# Contents

# Scorched!

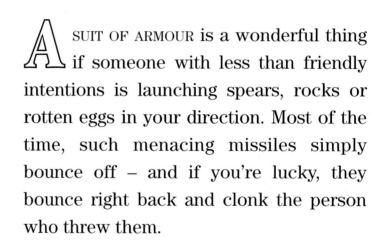

A SUIT OF ARMOUR is a wonderful thing if someone with less than friendly intentions is launching spears, rocks or rotten eggs in your direction. Most of the time, such menacing missiles simply bounce off – and if you're lucky, they bounce right back and clonk the person who threw them.

But if you wear armour when a dragon is showing an irritating interest, you are likely to feel as if you are sitting in a saucepan – and someone has turned the gas on. You start by feeling pleasantly warm, then unpleasantly warm, then horribly hot, then steam starts to come out of your poleyns – not a pretty sight.

Sir Bertilak Odorous, who had the misfortune to discover the fricasséed remains of his (admittedly unpleasant) uncle outside a dragon's cave in the Murky Mountains, was determined that such a fate would never befall *him*. He took himself off to the most famous inventor in the kingdom to commission an air-conditioned costume that would keep out lances, swords and other unsettling spikes but also be fire- and flame-proof.

Admittedly, the result looked odd. It wasn't easy to move in it, either, but that's a hazard of most suits of armour. Watching a knight in battle is like seeing a slow-motion action replay. Sir Bertilak decided that the suit must be tested before he would wear it. He looked about for a miserable menial who wouldn't make a fuss if slightly singed. His eye at once fell upon his unfortunate page, Porrit.

Now Porrit was poor, underfed and badly dressed, but he wasn't stupid. He knew perfectly well that dragon-proof-suit testing came high on the Most Dangerous Careers list. He pointed out in a most polite way that a suit built for a large and manly knight would not fit a little and boyish page.

Sir Bertilak snorted. The words "lily-livered pond scum" and "knock-kneed noodle" were some of the kinder ones he used. In short, he told Porrit that if he didn't climb into the suit straight away, he would be shoved in head first and have to make the most of it.

So it was that later that day an unhappy Porrit found himself sitting forlornly on a rock somewhere in the middle of the Murky Mountains. He was, of course, also in the middle of the dragon-proof armour. He was too short to see out of the visor and none of the bendy parts of the suit coincided with his own bendy parts, so moving was out of the question. All he could do was sit on his rock and wait for the worst. Namely, a dragon.

Now, it's a funny thing about dragons. You wait for years and years – sometimes for centuries and centuries – for one and never see the twitching of a scaly tail. Then three come along all at once.

That afternoon, it felt to Porrit as if the minutes were crawling past. It felt as if several other little things were crawling about inside his suit, too, but it's very hard to scratch yourself in over-sized armour. Pretty soon, Porrit was in agony.

The page didn't know what to do with himself. It felt as if every part of him itched, from his little toe to the top of his ears. He tried squiggling and wriggling around inside his suit. In the process, he fell right off his rock and found himself lying on his back like an overturned tortoise.

There was no way he could right himself.

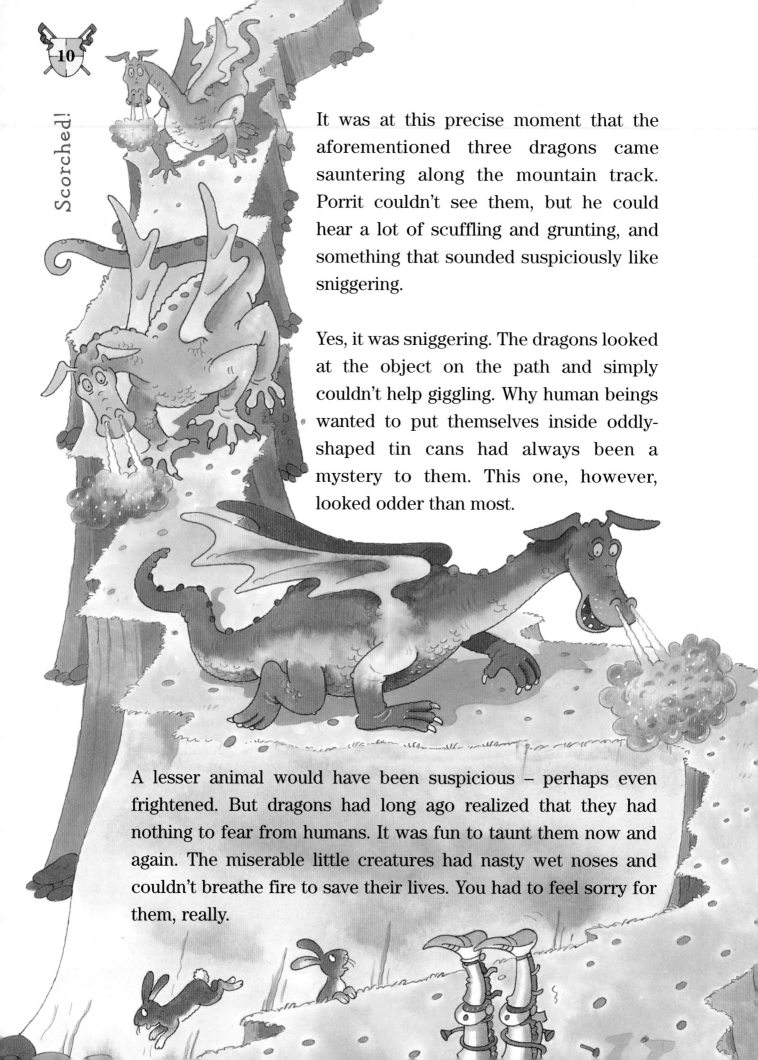

It was at this precise moment that the aforementioned three dragons came sauntering along the mountain track. Porrit couldn't see them, but he could hear a lot of scuffling and grunting, and something that sounded suspiciously like sniggering.

Yes, it was sniggering. The dragons looked at the object on the path and simply couldn't help giggling. Why human beings wanted to put themselves inside oddly-shaped tin cans had always been a mystery to them. This one, however, looked odder than most.

A lesser animal would have been suspicious – perhaps even frightened. But dragons had long ago realized that they had nothing to fear from humans. It was fun to taunt them now and again. The miserable little creatures had nasty wet noses and couldn't breathe fire to save their lives. You had to feel sorry for them, really.

The dragons' giggles subsided. They stood on the path in the sunshine looking at the object by their toes. Porrit, hearing only silence outside, kept very still. He waited. The dragons waited.

# *Thwummp!*

One of the dragons stopped waiting and leapt into action. He wondered what the strange shiny thing with the human in it would look like rolling down a mountainside.

From the dragons' point of view, it was marvellous. The suit of armour bounced from rock to rock, making a satisfying clanging sound with every impact.

From Porrit's point of view, it was probably the single most uncomfortable thing that had ever happened to him. And when you consider that he had worked for Sir Bertilak Odorous for five years, that's saying quite a lot.

*Oomph!* Porrit's head hit the inside of his helmet. *Thwack!* His knee bashed an outlet pipe. *Thud!* Two bendy bits of armour bent – but Porrit didn't.

A dauntingly dented suit of armour ricocheted down the mountain and into the valley below. It ended up, as luck would have it, at the foot of the mound on which Sir Bertilak's castle brooded. The battered article was carried into the castle and dropped without ceremony in the middle of the courtyard.

Both Sir Bertilak and the famous inventor peered down at it.

"Disappointing," murmured the inventor.

"Disastrous," growled Sir Bertilak.

No one gave a thought to the unfortunate inhabitant of the armour. It was only when he heard some wheezing sounds and a vague moaning that it occurred to the nasty knight to order the armour to be opened.

Many of the bystanders averted their eyes as the helmet of the suit was prised off. They were very much afraid that Porrit would emerge in more pieces than he went in.

Luckily, the page who was fished out of the mangled metal was still recognizably Porrit. He wouldn't have won any beauty contests and he was a little shaky on his legs, but all the essential bits were still present.

"Well?" demanded Sir Bertilak. "Did you meet any dragons, boy? Does the suit work?"

Porrit paused. He decided to start with the good news. "It is," he said, "fire-proof, flame-proof, singe-proof and scorch-proof ..."

"I knew it!" squealed the inventor.

"Ah-ha!" exclaimed Sir Bertilak, rubbing his hands together. A rosy future as an invincible dragon-slayer shimmered before him.

"The only thing is," said Porrit, "it isn't, it quite definitely isn't …dragon-proof."

Sir Bertilak did what Sir Bertilak does on occasions when his ire is aroused and his mood is malevolent. In short, he kicked Porrit up the stairs of one turret and down the stairs of another turret, finishing by hurling the protesting page into the murkiest corner of the moat. (You won't need a short course on castle sanitation to know that the moat was not exactly a wholesome place to be.)

Porrit reflected that, far from being dragon-proof, the suit wasn't even Sir Bertilak-proof. When he clambered, dripping and as odorous as his employer, from the moat, he somehow carelessly managed to leave the suit behind …

# Torched!

Huddled on the windward side of Sir Bertilak Odorous' castle was something even meaner and more miserable than the noisome knight. It was a village called Dump. And yes, it really was a dump. When Sir Bertilak's ancestors first built a small fort on the mound on the valley floor, they simply threw their rubbish over the battlements. After a few years, they had to wade through deer bones and discarded dishcloths every time they went in or out of the fort, so Tlac the Terrible (Sir Bertilak's great-great-great-great-great-great grandfather) decreed that in future rubbish should only be thrown in one direction.

Now, in medieval times (and still, some would say, today), where there's rubbish, there's a living to be made. It wasn't long before the growing dump below the growing castle became a scurvy scavenging-ground. Various unwholesome characters scurried about there day and night – and I'm not talking about the rats.

You might think that deer bones and discarded dishcloths would be of little use to anyone, but you'd be amazed (and probably appalled) by what can be done with them. One or two of the scurriers became rich enough to wear shoes. Then, one day, an eagle-eyed boy spotted something twinkling in the remains of a pig pie. In throwing the offending dish over his shoulder, the current lord had thrown a large gold and ruby ring at the same time. Its finder couldn't believe his luck.

Finders of gold and ruby rings often fondly believe that their new-found wealth can be kept a secret. It can't. Frankly, swanning around in a new set of rags is a bit of a give-away. Pretty soon, there were even more scurriers on the dump, as more and more young hopefuls came to try to make their fortunes.

It wasn't long before the traffic between the castle and the dump was squirming in both directions. The vile village was soon supplying the castle with everything from kitchen knaves to kitchen knives. Some historians even believe that it supplied the family name, as well. Nothing, after all, could be more odorous than Dump.

Which, now that you have had a brief history of that sorry collection of hovels, brings us back to the story. Sir Bertilak, not one to learn from experience, still has great ambitions to be a famous dragon-slayer. The problem, as I have hinted before, is that dragons are unpredictable and unco-operative creatures. They have, on the whole, more sense than to wander about on mountain passes crying, "Slay me! Slay me!"

Sir Bertilak hadn't actually seen a dragon in the last seventeen years, but it is hard to acquire a reputation for dragon-slaying in a dragon-drought. His habit, in times of crisis, was always to consult an expert. They may give useful information. At the very least, they are someone else to blame when things go wrong. When there is a lack of dragons, however, there tends to be a lack of dragon experts. Sir Bertilak was forced to fall back on an exceedingly ancient tome entitled: *Ye Booke of Dragones: all ye ever sought to know.*

Sir Bertilak was not a great reader. He settled down with a dozen capons and a hogshead of ale and threw the book at his page, Porrit. When Porrit had picked himself up out of the evil-smelling rushes on the floor, he began to read.

The book was a large one. For the next three days, Porrit read steadily on while Sir Bertilak, munched, quaffed, burped, snored and rumbled in the corner. By Wednesday evening, Porrit had gone through "Dragon Biology", "The Life-cycle of the Dragon", "Dragon Habitats", and "Dragon Migration: Fact or Fiction?" It wasn't until he came to "Hunting Dragons" that Sir Bertilak woke up and took notice.

Like many manuals of its day, *Ye Booke of Dragones* went into great detail about how to track the beasts in question. Both Porrit and his master learnt more about dragon droppings than they had ever wished to know. The method for finding out if a dropping was fresh was particularly disgusting and put Sir Bertilak off his haunch of venison for several minutes.

"Signs of Singing," read Porrit, moving swiftly on.

"Singing? Dragons don't sing!" bellowed Sir B.

"Sorry, sire," Porrit looked ahead. "I read it wrong. They don't sing. They singe."

The knight began to look interested. A couple of weeks earlier, one of the thatched hovels of Dump had gone up in flames. At the time, a cooking fire with one too many logs on it had been blamed, but suddenly Sir Bertilak wasn't so sure. What if a passing dragon had been the culprit? It was well known that dragons, especially in the summertime, could be careless with their breathing.

Sir Bertilak couldn't be bothered to listen to the rest of the book. He felt he was on to something. As usual when the loathsome lord had a bee in his bonnet, he didn't keep quiet about it. He sent out guards to every part of his lands asking for details of any recent fire, however small.

It was a fatal mistake. No one wanted to say they had nothing to report. The guards were large, loutish and armed. In settlements that had not had a fire for centuries, enterprising inhabitants made sure that a few flickering flames were soon (only slightly) out of control somewhere in the village.

Naturally, in some places the fires escaped from management and burned down a few homes in the process, but that can seem a small price to pay when a guard is parting your hair with his halberd.

Ever wishing to placate their lord and master, the foul folk of Dump set more fires than anyone else.

After a night on which half the hovels in Dump burned down, Sir Bertilak was in a fever of excitement.

"There's been no report of this level of dragon activity for centuries," he crowed. "And it's getting closer all the time. Tonight, Porrit, we'll lie in wait. Tomorrow, there'll be a scaly skin hanging from my battlements."

A man like Sir Bertilak doesn't suffer discomfort lightly. All that day, his minions rushed about setting up a luxurious camp right next to Dump. In fact, they set it up twice. The first time, with the wind in the wrong direction, evidence of the presence of Dump was all too strong. Even Sir Bertilak, not renowned for being fragrant, felt it was too much. The camp was rebuilt on the other side of Dump.

That night, after a good supper and with a hand-picked team around him just in case, Sir Bertilak ordered the lights in the camp to be doused. In darkness, he waited for the arrival of as many dragons as might decide to call.

Hours passed. The moon rose. But no snuffling, snorting or flapping of dragon wings disturbed the night. Sir Bertilak and his men had dozed off over their shields when a jaw-juddering shout went up.

# *Fire!*

A youngster from Dump, unaware that the fire-setting system had been suspended, had thrown an enthusiastic torch out of a window – right into the dragon-hunters' camp.

Next morning, looking slightly silly without his eyebrows, Sir Bertilak Odorous planned his next campaign. There was no doubt in his mind that a dastardly dragon had very nearly ambushed him the night before. The dragon must be dealt with.

He needed another plan …

# Toasted!

S IR BERTILAK PONDERED his dragon problem for some time. His forebears had also had a dragon problem, but theirs was a case of too many dragons, not too few. The ne'er-do-well knight needed to summon up at least one fire-breathing creature if his reputation as a dragon-slayer were to survive.

As Sir Bertilak fulminated in his
castle, clouds gathered overhead,
servants scuttled about, superstitious
and scared, while thunder roared (and
Sir Bertilak roared, too) and lightning flashed
(and Sir Bertilak hurled unsuspecting minions from
the windows). Trapped inside, the noisome knight
had no choice but to brood upon his lack of
performance in the death-to-dragons field. The only good
thing about the storm was that all the smouldering fires in
the countryside sizzled out. The bad thing was that all those
left homeless by recent conflagrations got very wet indeed.

The more he pondered, the more it seemed to Sir Bertilak that an expedition, uncomfortable and costly as this would be, was essential. Everyone knew that dragons lived in the Murky Mountains. Plumes of smoke could be seen coming from the highest peak from time to time, which was a sure sign. Instead of waiting for dragons to come to him, Sir Bertilak decided to go out and confront the risky reptiles in their lairs.

Naturally, young Porrit, the hapless page, was to be of the party. For one thing, he was the only person in the land who could read a map. Although the maps of the area were vague in the extreme, there was a very ancient one with exciting annotations. "Here be dragones," it said, in the middle of some pointy things meant to represent the Murky Mountains. It also said, "Here be man-eating frogs," near the Damp Swamp and "Here be headless giants," near the town of Gluggle, renowned for its ale shops.

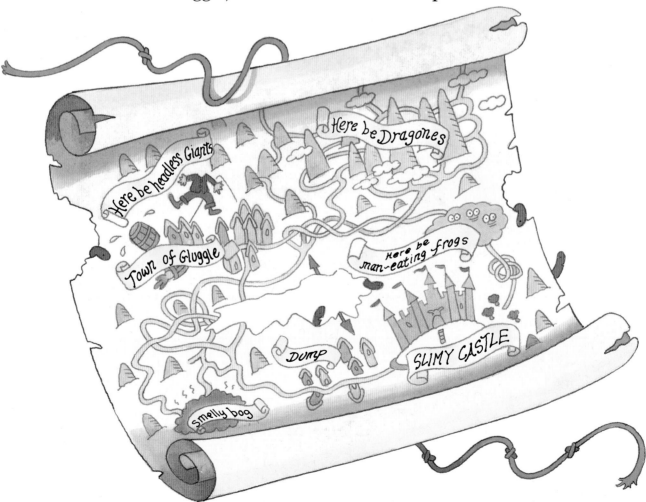

Sir Bertilak's impatience grew as the rain continued to fall, especially when it began to fall *inside* the castle. The roof had not been repaired for centuries. Why bother when you can simply order a minion to stand under each hole with a bucket? However, when drips become torrents, even the most willing minion with the biggest bucket is no use. Sir Bertilak cowered under a canopy and growled.

When the rain slowed to a few sulky drops, the Odorous one summoned his men and informed them that he wished to be ready to set out in an hour's time. He set his hourglass to underline the point. Sixty minutes later, the expedition, somewhat hastily prepared, set off. Needless to say, a number of essential items were left behind in the rush.

One of them was the map.

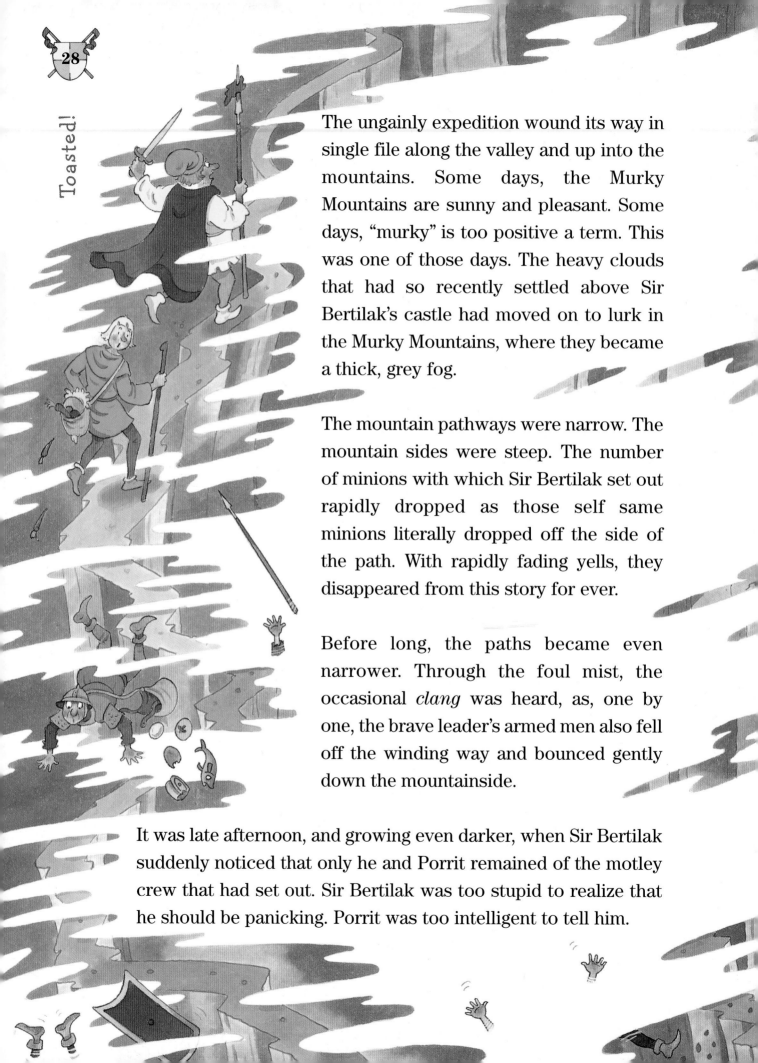

The ungainly expedition wound its way in single file along the valley and up into the mountains. Some days, the Murky Mountains are sunny and pleasant. Some days, "murky" is too positive a term. This was one of those days. The heavy clouds that had so recently settled above Sir Bertilak's castle had moved on to lurk in the Murky Mountains, where they became a thick, grey fog.

The mountain pathways were narrow. The mountain sides were steep. The number of minions with which Sir Bertilak set out rapidly dropped as those self same minions literally dropped off the side of the path. With rapidly fading yells, they disappeared from this story for ever.

Before long, the paths became even narrower. Through the foul mist, the occasional *clang* was heard, as, one by one, the brave leader's armed men also fell off the winding way and bounced gently down the mountainside.

It was late afternoon, and growing even darker, when Sir Bertilak suddenly noticed that only he and Porrit remained of the motley crew that had set out. Sir Bertilak was too stupid to realize that he should be panicking. Porrit was too intelligent to tell him.

"I suggest, sire," he ventured, "that we should rest in this cave until … until the rest of the party catches up with us."

"Sluggards!" sneered Sir Bertilak loudly. "Laggards! Slaggards!"

Porrit hurried his master into the cave before he could do any more damage to the English language.

It was surprisingly warm inside the cave. It was surprisingly light, too – almost as if there was a glow coming from the back of the rocky shelter.

Sir Bertilak, rapidly shedding clothes until an unwholesome amount of his flabby flesh was visible, began to rant about the subject that was always uppermost in his mind: dragons.

"Of course," he pontificated, "we might meet one at any time, but the likelihood is that they are all hiding. It's well known that dragons are lily-livered overgrown lizards, scared to show their faces when humans are around. They are cowardly creatures. No wonder it takes a man of my skills to hunt one down."

At some point during this speech, Porrit began to gesticulate wildly and make funny sounds in the back of his throat. Sir Bertilak took no notice, although he did begin to feel even hotter.

"Dragons aren't the creatures they're cracked up to be," the knight went on. "They're only slimy reptiles, after all. As for fire-breathing, well, I've seen circus tricksters do it. It's nothing to get worked up about."

In the next second, three important things happened. There was something that sounded very like a snort of derision. Sir Bertilak yelped as his greasy locks caught fire. And Porrit fainted.

The dragon, who had been sitting quietly in the back of the cave for some time, watched with amusement as Sir Bertilak rushed outside and stuck his head into a convenient mountain pool. She looked down with interest at young Porrit, who smelt vaguely familiar, before lolloping gently into the depths of the cave, leaving the intrepid hunters in the dark in more ways than one.

"Absolutely no need," growled the knight with the singed locks, "to mention this to anyone at all."

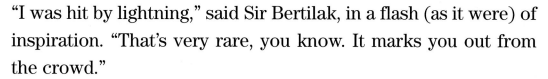

"Sorry, sire," said Porrit diplomatically. "I fainted and didn't see a thing. What did happen, exactly?"

"I was hit by lightning," said Sir Bertilak, in a flash (as it were) of inspiration. "That's very rare, you know. It marks you out from the crowd."

In Sir Bertilak's case, it certainly did. From that day, he sported a decidedly dodgy hair-do, which no amount of grooming could ever improve.

# Boiled!

Sir Bertilak Odorous and young Porrit spent the night in the cave. It seemed wiser than venturing out into fog that became murkier with every passing minute. The page did not sleep at all. Having had a good look at the unseen inhabitant of the rocky room, he felt that someone at least should keep watch. Sir Bertilak, who had now persuaded himself of the truth of his lightning story, had no such inhibitions. He snored happily through the night until a small boulder hit him heavily on the nose.

The would-be dragon-slayer was dazed for a moment. Then he leapt to his feet and shook his page vigorously.

"Not a very funny joke, Porrit!" he snarled, as his nose swelled to twice its usual size.

On balance, Porrit thought it better to take the blame than to reveal that a scalier hand than his own had probably thrown the missile. Besides, dawn was breaking on a crisp, clear day. It was time to go home.

The pair set off down the narrow path. Sir Bertilak grumbled and groaned without pause. Porrit was silent. Several important thoughts were chasing each other through his tired brain and causing him deep concern. Firstly, there was the narrowness of the path. Yesterday, in the fog, Porrit had been blissfully unaware of the yawning chasms at his feet. Now, every step seemed to cause him to sway dangerously over the edge.

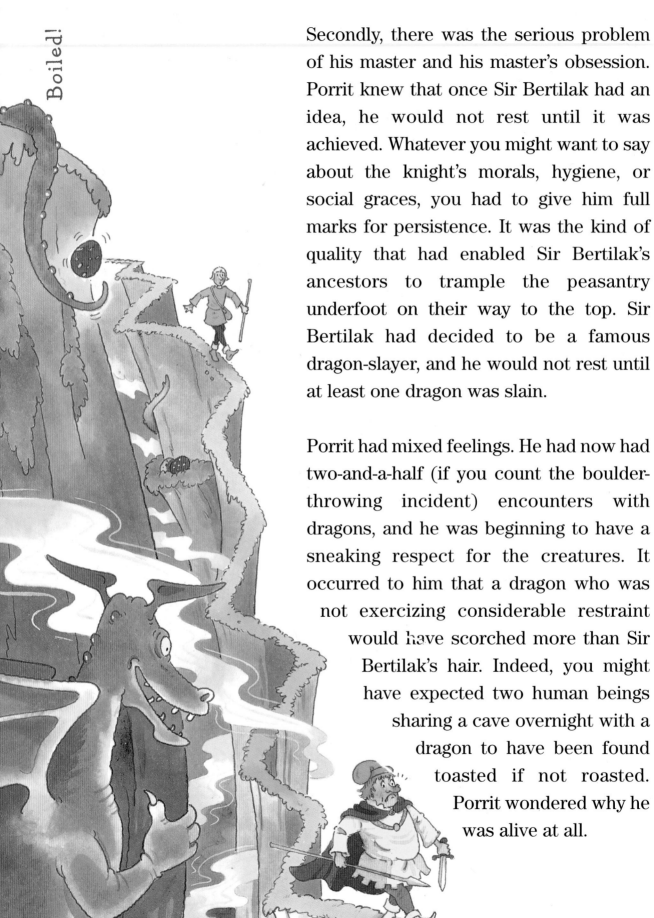

Secondly, there was the serious problem of his master and his master's obsession. Porrit knew that once Sir Bertilak had an idea, he would not rest until it was achieved. Whatever you might want to say about the knight's morals, hygiene, or social graces, you had to give him full marks for persistence. It was the kind of quality that had enabled Sir Bertilak's ancestors to trample the peasantry underfoot on their way to the top. Sir Bertilak had decided to be a famous dragon-slayer, and he would not rest until at least one dragon was slain.

Porrit had mixed feelings. He had now had two-and-a-half (if you count the boulder-throwing incident) encounters with dragons, and he was beginning to have a sneaking respect for the creatures. It occurred to him that a dragon who was not exercizing considerable restraint would have scorched more than Sir Bertilak's hair. Indeed, you might have expected two human beings sharing a cave overnight with a dragon to have been found toasted if not roasted. Porrit wondered why he was alive at all.

It was even stranger that the obnoxious Odorous one, whose views on dragons were hardly politically correct, had only a silly haircut to show for a night in the mountains.

Porrit was a loyal page. He followed his master through thick (no one could say that Sir Bertilak was the brightest button in the box) and thin (gruel, mostly). But Porrit's mind was much occupied, which is perhaps why, when he looked up, he was shocked to see that Sir Bertilak was no longer stomping along in front of him.

In horror, Porrit peered over the edge of the ledge. Surely he would have heard a body as solid as Sir Bertilak's thudding down the slope? It was hard to believe that the knight would have gone quietly. The page was forced to conclude that his master had taken a different path. Porrit turned around and, as quickly as he dared, retraced his steps around the mountainside.

It wasn't long before a strange sulphurous smell began to tickle his nostrils. It smelt as if something rotten was being burnt. Dread filled Porrit's humble heart. To be honest, it wasn't really that he feared for the health of Sir Bertilak. It was more that he felt a little squeamish about the sight that might meet his eyes. Sir Bertilak had, on more than one occasion, regaled his page with the story of how he had discovered his overcooked uncle outside a dragon's lair. The details had been gruesome in the extreme.

Porrit steeled himself to turn the next bend, behind which billows of smoke were wafting. Coughing and spluttering, he clung to the rock and prepared himself for a ghastly sight.

It was a ghastly sight indeed. A naked Sir Bertilak was cavorting in a steaming pool, fed by warm springs. His clothing, flung over nearby rocks, decorated the scene. Porrit gulped and averted his eyes. It was several months since Sir Bertilak had bathed. In the hot water and steam, his hairy hide had become the colour of a cooked lobster – but nothing like so appetizing.

"Come on in!" yelled Sir Bertilak. "And you can wash my clothes while you're about it!"

Porrit dutifully obeyed, but sensibly jumped in fully clad. He figured that his own clothes could get washed at the same time. Porrit worked for hours on Sir Bertilak's ghastly garments, while his master plunged and wallowed like a demented whale.

At last, with the clothes draped over the rocks to dry, Porrit sat down on the edge of the pool and, worn out after his sleepless night, fell fast asleep.

He was rudely awoken by bellowing. Sir Bertilak had lumbered from the water and was searching for his clothes. They were nowhere to be seen.

This time, Porrit hesitated to take the blame. Among the many pleasant things that Sir Bertilak was in the process of promising the perpetrator, being held upside-down in the steaming pool was one of the most appealing.

Porrit cleared his throat. "It is well known, Sire," he said, "that dragons often steal the clothes of those they fear. They hope it will diminish their strength and power."

Sir Bertilak paused in mid-rant. "Really?" he muttered. A silly smile spread across his face. "Porrit," he grinned, "we're getting somewhere at last! I can *smell* success! Let's get home and make proper preparations."

The pair trudged towards the castle. The broiled baron was no longer grumbling but humming happily (horribly, but happily) to himself. Porrit was dodging from rock to rock. One of the pair would be arriving home naked. You can bet your own buttocks it wasn't Sir Bertilak.

# Roasted!

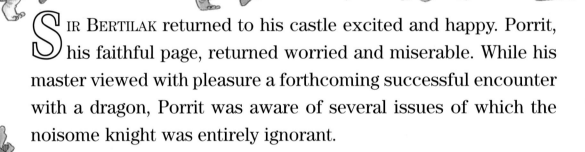

Sᴿ Bᴇʀᴛɪʟᴀᴋ returned to his castle excited and happy. Porrit, his faithful page, returned worried and miserable. While his master viewed with pleasure a forthcoming successful encounter with a dragon, Porrit was aware of several issues of which the noisome knight was entirely ignorant.

1. There were not just one or two dragons in the vicinity. The Murky Mountains were crawling with them.

2. The dragons were not, as Sir Bertilak believed, stupid and cowardly. They were clever and courageous.

3. Sir Bertilak was not, as he himself believed, clever and courageous. He was stupid and rashly stupid.

4. (And this was the worst point of all.) The dragons had a tremendous sense of fun.

While Sir Bertilak spent an uncomfortable couple of hours being squidged and squeezed into a new suit of clothes, Porrit sat on the least smelly bit of floor he could find and thought about everything that had happened. It didn't increase his cheeriness. When his master finally stomped into the room, his first words made Porrit feel even worse.

"Porrit!" roared Sir Bertilak, "I've had a thought!"

These unlikely words would make any page tremble. With growing terror, Porrit listened while his master expounded his peculiar ponderings.

"I've been thinking about the old stories, Porrit," said Sir Bertilak, sitting down heavily on an unsuspecting hound. "There's a lot of sense in some of those ancient tales. Do you know what we've been missing in all our quests?"

Several words sprang to mind. Intelligence? Common sense? Hygiene? "No, sire," muttered Porrit.

"That's why you're a paltry page and I'm a knight," replied Sir Bertilak with satisfaction. "The answer is staring you in the face. At least, it isn't staring you in the face. And that's the problem."

"You mean ...?" enquired Porrit, totally at sea but hoping he sounded as if he was understanding every word.

"Maidens!" hollered Sir Bertilak. "All the legends of the past have a maiden in them. You chain her up on a rock and, when the dragon turns up and eats her, you leap out and kill it."

"I think you're supposed to kill it *before* it eats the maiden," squawked Porrit.

"Before? After? What's the difference?" cried his master. "Now, who have we got we could chain to a rock?"

In truth, Sir Bertilak's history with maidens or any self-respecting woman had not been glorious. Most of them had the sense to keep out of his way. There was, in fact, only one suitable unfortunate female in the castle. Porrit shut his eyes and prayed that his master would not think of the obvious. It was to no avail.

"Agnes!" screeched Sir Bertilak. "Perfect! It's time that wretched girl made herself useful."

I should explain that Agnes was Sir Bertilak's niece, dumped on him by his brother, a knight second only to Sir Bertilak in general awfulness. Sir Slimeone had gone off to fight in the crusades (a hundred and fifty years after they were over). As his map-reading was as bad as his grasp of current affairs, he had sailed off in entirely the wrong direction. His arrival in North America is unrecorded by the history books, as is his encounter with an unfriendly bear – a meeting that could only be described as grisly.

Agnes was a sensible girl and did her best to avoid the notice of her uncle. She had not, however, avoided the notice of Porrit, who was inclined to think that she was the most angelic creature ever to place her perfumed foot upon the blossoming earth. (She did not, in fact, have perfumed feet – far from it – but that was the way Porrit thought about her.)

Porrit was panicking now. He begged Sir Bertilak to consider the foul mood Sir Slimeone might be in if he returned to find his daughter roasted by a reptile. The knight was not impressed. Out of sight was out of mind in his book, and anyway, he thought it unlikely that his brother would ever return. In this he was, very unusually, correct.

Before Porrit could think of another argument, the protesting girl was dragged before her uncle.

"Agnes," said Sir Bertilak with a smile that struck horror into the hearts of all that saw it, "I thought we might go for a little picnic in the country. Let's see. Where would be pleasant at this time of year? Hmmm. Oh, I know! The Murky Mountains! Go and get your cloak, my dear."

Agnes was a level-headed and intelligent girl. If the gruesome leer on her uncle's face and the unexpectedness of the invitation had not worried her, the sight of Porrit, pale and trembling as if he had seen a ghost, would have alarmed her a great deal. Thoughtfully, she returned to her chamber and tucked a number of potentially useful items into her clothing before joining her uncle in the courtyard.

The picnic party set out. Agnes wondered why her uncle felt it necessary to wear full armour. She wondered why the mule carrying the food made a clanking sound as it walked. She wondered why Porrit, who usually gazed at her with pitiful adoration, now couldn't look at her at all. Agnes tightened her grip on a small dagger hidden up her sleeve and kept her wits about her.

For once the Murky Mountains were anything but murky. The sun beat down as the small party, consisting of Sir Bertilak, Agnes, Porrit and a couple of men-at-arms, wound its way through the foothills. By the time the party had reached the higher peaks, Sir Bertilak was positively steaming. The heat and the suit of armour resulted in a kind of pressure-cooker effect. He felt more and more uncomfortable.

"It's no good," came a muffled roar at last, "I can't keep this stuff on. I'll roast in here. Let me out!"

Porrit knew that it would take some time to extricate big Sir Bertilak from his armour. This might be the only chance. He casually wandered past Agnes on her palfry and whispered out of the side of his mouth, "Watch for your chance. Escape! Go!"

"What?" asked Agnes. "Speak up, I can't hear you!"

Porrit raised his voice a fraction and added to it an expression of such doleful pleading that there was no doubting his meaning. Agnes was no fool. She gripped her reins and prepared for flight.

Meanwhile, Porrit was beginning to wrestle with Sir Bertilak's helmet. "Now!" he yelled.

Alas, the shout, Agnes's enthusiastic kicks and the heat of the day had a bad effect on the paltry palfry. It neighed. It reared. It kicked out with all four feet and took off at the speed of light down a mountain track no wider than Agnes's unperfumed foot. Meanwhile, two men-at-arms, a hapless page and an over-armed knight, having been heavily hit by a flying hoof each, flew through the air with the greatest of ease. Where will they fall? Will Agnes become a dragon's dinner? Do belligerent Bertilaks bounce? For the answer to these and many other questions, turn the page …

# Simmered!

FOR SEVERAL SECONDS strange sounds echoed around the mountains. There was the *clang! clang! CLANG!* as a large knight in armour ricocheted down a steep valley. There was bad language of the worst possible kind bouncing from rocky cliff to stony steep (also from the large knight). There was the clatter of hooves as a high-spirited horse thundered off in another direction entirely, leaving its rider to roll elegantly down a slope that looked suspiciously like the inside of the crater of a volcano. There was a weird wailing from a page who, from an upside-down position wedged between two boulders, saw the light of his life vanishing in the direction of an agonising end. From the two men-at-arms there was a *clonk! clonk!* as they both hit their heads on a rock, followed by an ominous silence.

As the echoes faded away with a *clang! pustules! clop! wah! clonk!* Porrit unwedged himself with difficulty and waited while the blood rushed back to his boots. In such a situation, a page's duty is to his master. Porrit knew perfectly well that what he *should* do was to clamber carefully down to the ledge far below where he could see something like a large, shiny beetle waving its legs in the air. At any moment, Sir Bertilak might become dislodged and plummet to his doom.

Porrit, as we know, was a faithful page, but his heart was hurtling down a volcano with the woman of his dreams and he had to follow it. Ignoring the bellowing beetle below, he set off down a perilous path towards dark and steamy depths.

Meanwhile, Agnes was having a rather interesting time. As she rolled towards certain death, her skirts caught on an outcrop of rock. She found herself inelegantly hanging just above the entrance to a cave. By swinging and wriggling, she eventually managed to tear herself free from her skirts and drop down into the mouth of the cave.

At first sight, the cave appeared to be empty, but an eerie glow towards the back encouraged the intrepid maiden to explore. As she crept forward, she was surprised to hear, faintly at first, then louder and louder, an extraordinary kind of music.

Five hundred years before its appearance among human beings, rock and roll was wildly popular among dragons. (It was named, of course, after the round stony stuff they found all around them and what happened if you gave it a hearty shove down a mountainside.)

Agnes peered around a corner, her eardrums pulsating, and found herself in a vast cavern, where four dragons were entertaining an excessively excited crowd of young reptiles.

Meanwhile, back on the ledge, or rather, on his back on the ledge, Sir Bertilak, who earlier, you remember, had felt unwelcomingly warm in his armour, was now positively poached. The sun shone down on his shiny breastplate, toasting his tummy within. The knight grew hotter and hotter, and crosser and crosser. He hollered for his page until he was hoarse. He swore and cursed until the rocks around him turned red. But no one came.

Sir Bertilak, unable to see anything but the searing sky above him through the visor of his helmet, which had wedged shut, had no idea that he was lying on a very narrow ledge. The ledge was, in fact, a good deal more narrow than the knight. If he had known, Sir Bertilak might not have wriggled so wrathfully …

*CLANG! CLUNK! KER-CLONG! BOING! SPLASSSSHHHHHH!* Sir Bertilak jiggled himself off his ledge and descended a thousand feet or so at astonishing speed. At the bottom, he found himself sitting in a small mountain pool of delicious coolness. Steam rose around him as he quietly (for once) cooled. His helmet had come off in the fall (Sir Bertilak made a mental note to have his armourer's guts for garters in an all-too-literal sense), and a broad smile filled the knight's foolish face as he felt coolness reach parts that had been disturbingly simmered.

Life for Porrit was less blissful at that moment. His skirts being shorter than Agnes's, he did not get caught on the protruding rock but instead knocked first his knee and then his head with a sickening thwack. He felt as if he were falling from a great height (well, he *was* falling from a great height but he now felt it even more), and the world suddenly went black.

A couple of hundred feet further into the mountain, Agnes was crouching behind a rock and observing the scene before her. She hardly knew what to feel most shocked about – the sight of a huge group of dragons (when she had never seen a single one in her life before) or the sound of rock and roll (when she had only ever heard tedious troubador songs and Sir Bertilak's hunting bellows before). It was a lot for a girl to take in.

Just as Agnes's heart was beginning to thump a little less (it may, in any case, have been confused with the driving beat being laid down by the dragons' drummer), she found she had something worse to worry about. A large hand was placed firmly on her shoulder and she felt hot breath on the back of her neck.

For an awful moment, Agnes thought that Sir Bertilak had caught up with her. She looked down. In an even more awful moment, she realized that the hand was distinctly scaly.

Agnes, as you know, had no experience of dealing with dragons. Swiftly, she reviewed her options:

1. She could stab the creature with her dagger or any one of the other small implements she had brought with her.

2. She could try to engage the dragon in conversation and appeal to its better instincts.

3. She could fall down and pretend to be dead.

Just as swiftly, Agnes dismissed the first two options.

1. Her dagger was very small. The dragon was very large. It would be like stabbing Sir Bertilak with a darning needle. It wouldn't kill him and it wouldn't do much for his temper.

2. She had no idea if dragons understood English. Worse, she had no idea if dragons had better instincts.

The dragon leaned over and looked into Agnes's face. He sighed, singeing the maiden's eyebrows. Agnes had no need to choose option 3. She fainted, and it chose itself.

What is not generally known is that dragons often have as little experience of how to deal with maidens as maidens have of how to deal with dragons.

The dragon thought a bit and looked closely at Agnes, singeing more of her hair in the process.

He wondered if she was cold, and breathed even more heavily, completing the singeing process.

Finally, he picked her up and carried her off to a cool cave where she would keep fresh while he consulted his mother.

It was only a few minutes before Agnes awoke. She felt a little chillier. She would have felt chillier still if she had known she was in the dragon equivalent of a fridge.

It was gloomy in the cave. Agnes waited until her eyes grew used to the dark and noticed a lumpy shape on the other side of the space. The longer she sat in the silence, the more convinced she became that the lumpy shape was breathing, but with her ears still throbbing from the dragons' disco, she couldn't be sure.

There was only one thing to do. Agnes crawled cautiously across the cave, peering through the gloom. It looked like … it couldn't be … it was strangely like …

# "Aaaaaaaaaaaaaaagh!"

screamed Agnes, startled by a badly bruised Porrit.

# "Aaaaaaaaaaaaaaagh!"

screeched Porrit, horrified by a terribly toasted Agnes.

When they had regained their composure, the hapless pair explained to each other what had happened since they had last been together. It seemed like hours ago but was, in fact, a mere seven minutes.

Porrit was trembling with relief that his beloved had been found, even if her hairstyle was now a little extreme, but he suddenly found himself breathless and red in the face.

"What is it?" asked Agnes. "Are you going to faint?"

"N-n-n-n-no," stammered Porrit. "It's … it's … you're showing your l-l-l-legs!" He had never seen a maiden's legs before and felt strongly that he shouldn't be seeing them now."

"Oh, for goodness sake!" cried Agnes, when she realized what the problem was. "How did you think I got around?"

This interesting conversation was rudely interrupted by the arrival of the dragon who had found Agnes and his mother, not best pleased to be dragged away from her dancing.

Now dragons speak a very ancient language. It combines prehistoric grunts and squeals with a high-pitched wailing. What is not generally known is that after hundreds of years of rock and roll, most dragons have hardly any hearing left at all. Although the grunts and squeals still go on, they mainly communicate by lip-reading.

Porrit and Agnes cowered in a corner while the dragon and his mother made extraordinary noises at each other. The cave was, of course, no longer gloomy, as the fiery breath of the related reptiles gave an eerie red glow.

The humans had no idea what was being said, which was probably just as well. Here is a translation.

*Mother: You dragged me away for THIS?*

*Son: Sorry. I didn't know what to do with it. And now it's multiplying!*

*Mother: What are you talking about? I threw this other one in here myself five minutes ago. It fell on me on my way to the concert. It wasn't awake then.*

*Son: So what are we going to do with them?*

*Mother: Humans are pretty feeble. If we leave them here they'll start to go off. We can eat them or throw them into the volcano.*

*Son: Do they taste good?*

*Mother: Try a bit, if you like. I ate one of the shiny ones once, but it was a bit crunchy and bits got stuck in my teeth. You might need to fillet them first. Jeep Cherokee. (Note: I think the translator got confused here. Although dragons had rock and roll well before humans, they certainly were not clever with four-wheel-drive vehicles.)*

*Son: Oh, let's just leave them. It sounds like too much trouble.*

*Mother: Boom, chugga, boom, chugga, wah, wah, wah. Come ON! I love this song …*

With that, the dragons waddled away.

"Let's get out of here," said Porrit, which was the most sensible thing he had said for some time. Hand in hand, he and Agnes crept out of the cave.

Ever been lost in a mountain? The pair wisely turned away from the throbbing of the bass beat, but that meant they were wandering deeper into the cave system. This would have been even more difficult if Agnes had not retrieved a flint and a torch from somewhere about her person. By its weak and flickering light, they went on.

There were curious drawings on the walls, from which Agnes and Porrit might have learnt much if they had stopped to look at them. There were horrible rumblings and hissings from underground vents. There were stalagmites and stalactites placed exactly at forehead and big-toe height.

At last, glimmering in the distance, a faint light appeared. Agnes and Porrit quickened their pace. To the page's disappointment, Agnes let go of his hand and strode on ahead. Seeing, quite literally, the light at the end of the tunnel had raised her spirits.

The entrance, when they reached it, was bathed in bright sunshine. Porrit and Agnes blinked and for a moment were unable to see where they were. Then an all-too-familiar voice boomed out from somewhere horribly close.

"Ye snipes and little swillins, what have you done to yourself, girl? No dragon's going to want you now!"

It was Sir Bertilak Odorous, sitting on a rock above a pool with his armour gently rusting into a kind of shell. He was hungry. He was angry. He was no further forward in his mission. In short, he needed someone to blame.

As usual, Porrit was perfect.

# Poached!

THE LANGUAGE USED BY SIR BERTILAK ODOROUS to his unfortunate page was appalling. He ignored the presence of Agnes, who would have raised her eyebrows at some of the words used if she had still had eyebrows. More to the point, the noisome knight ignored the presence of dragons. Of course, he was the only member of the company who still hadn't met a dragon, but all that was very shortly to change …

High above, among the rocky peaks, a couple of dragons we have met before were taking the air. It would never have occurred to them to peer down into the deep crevice beneath if it hadn't been for the booming and badgering coming from below. Dragons, as you know, do not hear well, but Sir Bertilak was venting his anger at a vicious volume. Furthermore, the crevice acted as a kind of natural megaphone, funnelling the sound to the ears of the scaly ones above.

I will spare you the words of Sir Bertilak. (It would not, in any case, be legal for me to print them on this page.) The words of the dragons, however, can safely be recorded. Again, the following passage is a translation.

*Son: Hey! Look down there! Isn't that ...?*

*Mother: Hmmm. Maybe. But you're right. They do seem to be multiplying. The baby looks huge. And it's one of the shiny ones. No good to us at all.*

*Son: Why does it have to make so much noise?*

*Mother: Babies are like that. Look, I'm fed up with this. Use your initiative. Make it stop.*

The younger dragon considered for a moment scrambling down the rocky crevice and flame-grilling the humans, but it seemed like too much effort. Instead, he picked up a handy rock and threw it into the depths.

None of the humans below heard the approaching missile, but Porrit chose that moment to seize his beloved and cover her ears, thereby pulling her out of the line of fire. A second later, Sir Bertilak felt the full force of the reptile's rock. It volleyed from his vambrace; it bounced from his breastplate; it pounded painfully on one of his poleyns.

## Boing! Bong! Bing!

Sir Bertilak was too shocked to speak for a moment, but far above, the dragons had become strangely interested.

*Son: Did you hear that? It sounded great! Banana laundry! (Sorry. Another translation problem, I think. Presumably this is some kind of slang Dragonese that is difficult to convey in modern English.)*

*Mother: You're right. Try it again.*

Another rock followed the first and hurtled into the depths. This time, it ricocheted from Sir Bertilak's rotund tummy, veered back onto the vambrace and plopped even more painfully down to his pulsating poleyn.

# Bong! Boing! Bing!

Sir Bertilak's fury knew no bounds. The adjectives he used about avalanches were utterly awful. But his excitement didn't begin to match that of the lizard-like listeners above.

*Son: That's fantastic! It's just what we've been looking for. A brilliant new sound!*

*Mother: I can't wait to hear more!*

And she did. Thirty-four rocks of various sizes came hurtling down the mountain. After the first nine, Sir Bertilak became strangely quiet, and Porrit and Agnes hid their eyes.

A symphony of sounds filled the Murky Mountains and suddenly the sound of enthusiastic applause echoed through the valleys. Porrit and Agnes looked up and saw to their astonishment that every ledge was packed with dragons, all drawn to the percussive sound of rocks hitting rogue.

Porrit's knees were shaking, but he felt he should try to be masterful.

"Don't move," he whispered to his true love, holding her close.

"Stop spitting in my ears!" hissed Agnes, who was far too interested in the dragons to feel the romance of the situation.

Neither Porrit nor Agnes needed to worry. Focusing on the best bit of drum kit to make its way to the Murky Mountains for many a millennium, the dragons took no notice at all of a couple of cowering humans. Several of them clambered down to Sir Bertilak's rock and lifted him off it, being particularly careful not to breathe on any part that looked as though it might be tuneful. As Porrit and Agnes watched, open-mouthed, the rapacious reptiles bore Sir Bertilak, now moaning faintly, away. The last they saw of him was the glint of his greaves as he was carried into a cave.

Not a scrap of scaly skin, not a hint of horny head, not a flicker of flaring flame remained to be seen. Porrit and Agnes looked around. Then they looked at each other.

"Did that," murmured Porrit, "really happen?"

Agnes nodded. "Look!"

Lying by the pool was Sir Bertilak's much-bashed helmet, which he had removed when the sun beat down. Porrit picked it up.

"We should go and look for him," he said. "I'm sure *The Page's Handbook* would say it was my duty to rescue my master from danger of every kind. Probably," he went on miserably, "that includes kidnap by dragons."

"Probably," Agnes agreed flatly.

The pair exchanged a long and meaningful look. Neither spoke but a great deal was going on in both their minds. Agnes was thinking, "Porrit wouldn't look bad in a blue jerkin. I wonder where my uncle hid my jewels? It's probably much too late to save him now. I'm hungry." (Remember, she *was* related to the nasty nobleman.)

Porrit was thinking, "Your eyes are like pools of sparkling sapphire. I wonder if you'd clonk me on the head if I said so. It's probably much too late to save him now. I'm hungry." (Remember, he'd had a very trying day.)

And so, hand in hand, Agnes and Porrit began the long walk back to the castle, feeling, although neither said a word, curiously in tune. And, speaking of tunes, if their thoughts had not been elsewhere, they might have heard, wafting through the valleys, a strangely melodious sound:

# Done!

IT TOOK SOME TIME for Porrit and Agnes to reach Castle Odorous. This was partly because they were now on foot instead of on steed, but mainly because they kept stopping for what poets at the time called dalliance. There is no need for us to dwell here on the details of such dalliance. Suffice it to say that the last thing Porrit was thinking about was the strange wailing that wafted on the wind from the Murky Mountains.

Neither Porrit nor Agnes had given much thought to their homecoming. Vaguely, each had imagined trudging up the castle mound and going back to life as usual. They were surprised, therefore, as they approached the lurking hovels of Dump, to see a huge crowd milling and melling beneath the mound.

As Porrit and Agnes approached, the crowd grew silent. The pair kept walking, but both developed an unattractive eye-swivelling habit as they tried to work out what was going on. Neither quite realized that they were hardly, after their adventures in the mountains (not to mention their dalliance in the dales), looking their best.

Done!

The crowd swirled and squirmed like a pot of soup going off the boil. Finally, a pink and portly man-at-arms was pushed forward. He appeared to be some kind of spokesperson.

"This official gathering …" he began.

"Fish gathering! Fish gathering!" muttered the crowd in agreement.

"This official gathering," the knight went on, "has been convened to decide what to do if … er … if the party that went into the Murky Mountains was … er … sadly …  er … never to return."

"Oh," said Porrit.

Agnes's reply was crisper. "But we have returned," she snapped.

"Butter turned. Butter turned." There was further muttering from the crowd.

The man-at-arms pulled himself together and got to the heart of the matter. "Not," he said, "all of you."

Porrit licked his lips nervously. He felt that someone was about to accuse him of losing something important. He couldn't think of a single decent excuse. How many pages carelessly mislay their lords and masters on a perfectly straightforward dragon-slaying expedition? Porrit gulped and decided it was best to get it over and done with.

"Our liege lord," he stammered, "has been kidnapped."

There was an ugly silence from the crowd.

"Not dead then?" asked the man-at-arms grimly.

The silence had now distinctly lost its looks.

"Not dead *as such*," replied Porrit. "Not dead the last time I caught sight of his … er … noble countenance."

The temperature dropped by several degrees. The man-at-arms persisted.

"He was in danger? Grave danger?"

Porrit knew the time had come to confess.

"Very grave danger," he said, expecting at any moment to be torn limb from limb. "The worst danger that any knight could be in. And I ... I left him there."

# Hooray!

An enormous roar rose from the crowd. Suddenly, hats, babies and the occasional granny were being hurled into the air. There was dancing. There was singing. There was kissing of inappropriate parties. There was a scene of jubilation, the like of which was unknown in the annals of Dump.

Porrit found himself lifted and carried triumphantly into the throng (where he was at some danger from flying hats, babies and grannies). Then the man-at-arms roared for silence and tried to compose his face.

"Then … with deep, deep sadness, of course … we must find a new lord."

All eyes turned to Porrit.

"What? Me?" Porrit was astonished. But the more he thought about it, the more he liked the idea. He saw himself vividly, dressed rather more elegantly than Sir Bertilak's style, partaking of a few choice sweetmeats and exchanging smiles with his lovely, delicate and delicious lady.

# *Not so fast!*

The roar came from the lovely, delicate and delicious lady herself. Porrit gasped to see the furious expression of his beloved. She was purple with rage. In fact, she reminded him strongly of someone. He just couldn't think who …

Agnes was speaking and speaking with passion. "I would remind you," she bellowed, "that I am the niece of Sir Bertilak Odorous, and as such, next in line. I claim this castle and all it contains. And you!" she finished as an afterthought, glaring at the inhabitants of Dump.

The crowd seethed and rumbled before sorting itself at last into two parties. The Porrit faction continued to carry him aloft but was becoming uncomfortably aware that he was, after all, only a page. On the other hand, at least he wasn't a woman! There had hardly been a lady at Castle Odorous for four hundred years (a fact not entirely unconnected with the ghastliness of the lords). The Agnes faction, which would have raised her aloft if she hadn't thwacked it on its heads with a stick, was uncomfortably aware that she was, after all, only a woman. On the other hand, at least she had spirit.

Porrit was eventually deposited by his supporters and found himself face-to-face with his rival. She glared. He glared … and found himself thinking about sapphire pools and sweetmeats again. Even Agnes found herself softening as she looked at Porrit's smitten smile. A solution to the whole problem suddenly occurred to her. She looked meaningfully at Porrit.

Done!

Telepathy had never been Porrit's strongest subject but suddenly, as he gazed into Agnes's eyes, the same thought came into his head. He tried to think of some elegant, memorable words in which to express himself.

"Why don't you marry the baggage?" cried his own faction, before he could speak.

"Get spliced to the shrimp!" shouted the Agnes crowd.

"Well, if I must," muttered Agnes.

"For the good of my people," replied Porrit grandly.

Time passed, as time will, and life at Castle Odorous gradually changed. Porrit discovered in himself a talent for interior decoration and redesigned the rooms from dungeons (now *much* more uncomfortable) to turrets (now terrifically tasteful).

Agnes occupied herself with her uncle's finances, and found them pleasantly healthy. She instituted a number of improvements in Dump and the surrounding area, with the result that the place is now hardly recognisable. Indeed, after Lady Agnes's Plumbing Reform Edict, the village decided that it deserved a new name, and the Kalitreb Garden Suburb was born.

On cold winter nights, when the wind howls around the (fully insulated) turrets, Porrit sometimes finds himself wondering if the wailing he can hear is really weather-related. Could there, perhaps, deep in the caves of the Murky Mountains, still be a resident percussion instrument that longs to come home?

Sometimes, Porrit decides at once to organize a rescue mission. He even makes a few notes on the back of a paint chart, but in the morning, a mission no longer seems such a good idea. No one goes to the Murky Mountains these days, and Porrit has warned his sons that the creatures who lurk there are too horrible to describe (and he isn't thinking of dragons).

No dragon's skin decorates Porrit's rooms. No dragon's head leers down from his walls. But both Porrit and Agnes have warm feelings about these scaly creatures – as their newly designed coat of arms reveals …

# AMAZING

# DRAGONS

# Ye sluggard!

NOT A VERY POLITE WAY to get your attention, I'm afraid, but the kind of language you will need to get used to if you are determined to read further. The above is by no means the nastiest name-calling in this sorry collection of stories, and the awful oaths of Sir Bertilak Odorous are only some of the horrors you'll meet.

In the first story, we meet several dragons and hear of a knight roasted in his armour. The second tale has fewer dragons but many instances of arson. Dragons are back in story three, and lots of knights fall off a mountain. In the next story, Sir Bertilak removes his clothes – the most horrible event in the book so far. Story five introduces a girl whose father's end was grisly (yes, a bear was involved). The remaining stories feature close encounters with dragons and smelly serfs – it's hard to say which is worse. The fate of Sir Bertilak Odorous, however, is particularly unpleasant.

You have been warned! Read on at your peril …